The Littles
Take a Trip

To Jennifer
John Peterson '88

BY JOHN PETERSON
PICTURES BY ROBERTA CARTER CLARK

SCHOLASTIC INC.
New York Toronto London Auckland Sydney

ISBN 0-590-40136-X

12 11 10 9 8 7 6 5 4 3 2   6 7 8 9/8 0 1/9
                                            11
Printed in the U.S.A.

To B de R

TOM LITTLE and his sister, Lucy, were not invited to Henry Bigg's birthday party. But they went anyway. They always went to Henry's parties. They had gone to them for as far back as they could remember.

Henry didn't know that Tom and Lucy were there. They watched from a secret look-out place above the dining-room door.

Tom and Lucy were the children of Mr. and Mrs. William T. Little. All the Littles were tiny people. They weren't midgets or dwarfs or even elves. They were tinier than that. Mr. Little was the tallest Little. And he was only six inches tall. All the other Littles were shorter than he was.

The Little family lived in the walls of the house owned by the Bigg family. Their ten small rooms took up only a little space. The Bigg family didn't know the Littles were living with them. The tiny people always kept out of sight.

Except for being tiny, the Littles looked and acted like ordinary people. The Littles were different in one way only: they had tails.

The Littles' tails weren't used for anything. They couldn't hang by their tails or use them to swat flies. But they were handsome tails, and the Littles were

proud of them. They kept them combed and brushed. And the women curled their tails and often wore ribbons on them.

As Tom and Lucy watched Henry Bigg and his friends, Lucy said, "They look silly without tails." She started giggling and couldn't stop.

"Be quiet!" said Tom Little. "They might hear you."

"I can't help it," said Lucy. She held her hand over her mouth.

"Besides, it's not important," said Tom. "Their not having tails, I mean."

"If it's not important, then why do *we* have them?" said Lucy.

"Because we do, that's all," said Tom. "We're the same as they are, only smaller. People are people."

"No we're not the same," said Lucy. "If we were, we'd have parties too, and invite friends to come."

When Lucy said that, Tom forgot he was having fun watching Henry Bigg's party. His sister was right. Tom and Lucy never saw any children their age and size. Of course Tom and Lucy were good friends. They really liked each other. But both of them wanted more than anything to have a friend outside of the family.

Tom, who was ten years old, wanted to play astronaut and other boys' games with a boy his age. And Lucy, age eight, longed to have a girl friend to play house with and to talk to.

Even so, Tom and Lucy weren't exactly lonely. Sometimes Uncle Pete played with them as if he were a boy. That was fun. And Granny Little was teaching Lucy all she knew about sewing and knitting, which was all there *was* to know.

But today Tom and Lucy were watching Henry Bigg's birthday party and feeling sorry for themselves. "You're right, Lucy," said Tom. "We must be different from Henry Bigg, because we never play with any other children."

"It's not fair," said Lucy. "Cousin Dinky gets to see all the other families. Why can't we?"

"Cousin Dinky is an *adventurer*," said Tom. "Dad says he takes a lot of chances. He could get killed."

"I thought you said you wanted to be just like Cousin Dinky when you grew up?"

"I do," said Tom. "But I'm not grown up yet."

"Anyway," said Lucy, "if there were another family like ours living in the Biggs' house with us, it wouldn't be so lonely. Why do we have to live so far away from the other tiny families? I hate it."

"Oh well, we have to," said Tom. "There's not supposed to be more than one family to a house. Dad's told us a hundred times. That way the big people will probably never find out about any of us."

"I don't see what's so important about that," said Lucy.

"Golly, Lucy — don't be silly," said Tom. "That's *very* important. They might not like the way we take the things we need from them, like food and everything."

"What would happen if they knew about us?"

"Maybe they'd put us in a museum," said Tom, "or a *circus*."

"So what?" said Lucy. "At least that would be more exciting than sitting here and watching."

"And maybe they'd kill us," said Tom. "They might think we were some kind of animal." He looked at his tail.

"Kill us?" said Lucy.

"Well, maybe," said Tom. "Gee — I don't really know what they'd do. I . . . I'm sorry I said that. They probably wouldn't *kill* us."

"Oh Tom," said Lucy. "I did a terrible thing. I gave Henry Bigg a birthday card. Now they'll find out about us and kill us."

"You what?" said Tom. He jumped up.

"I made a birthday card for Henry," said Lucy. "It's there." She pointed. "On that table in the Biggs' dining room. The one with the presents."

"Did you write anything on it? Did you tell him about us?"

"Not on the card, no," said Lucy.

"Well, at least you had that much sense."

"But I did in the letter I wrote."

"Letter! What letter?"

"I put a letter on the table too, Tom. Will we all be killed? Oh Tom!"

Tom Little dashed from the look-out place and ran to the tin-can elevator. (The Littles had made an elevator from a soup can and some pieces of string.) The boy rode in the elevator down to the dining-room floor.

Tom pushed open a secret door and walked into the Biggs' dining room. Tom was standing under the small table with the presents. He looked at the children. They were busy playing Pin the Tail on the Donkey. Tom climbed the electric cord of the table lamp without being seen.

The table top was covered with presents and birthday cards. Tom looked through the envelopes as quickly as he could. It wasn't easy. Most of the cards were bigger than he was. As he looked, Tom kept an eye on the children. One of the boys had just tried to pin the donkey's tail on Mrs. Bigg.

At last Tom found his sister's letter.

He snatched it up. Now where was the birthday card?

Mrs. Bigg spoke. "That's enough games for a while, children," she said. "Now let's open the presents. Then we can have cake and ice cream."

When Tom heard that, he jumped into a pot of English ivy that was on the table. He hid behind the leaves. "Why," thought Tom, "why oh why am I wearing a red shirt instead of a green one?" He wrapped himself in a leaf.

Poor Tom Little! He had to stay hidden in that pot of English ivy until Henry Bigg opened all his cards and presents.

Tom hoped that Lucy was watching. All this trouble was her fault.

"How strange," said Mrs. Bigg when Henry got to Lucy's card. "It's so tiny, and it's homemade."

"Who's Lucy Little?" said Henry Bigg.

Nobody knew, of course.

"That's crazy," said Henry. He went on to the other cards and presents.

Later Lucy told Tom she was awfully sorry, and would he please not tell Mother and Daddy? She would never do it again. Tom said he would think it over. He didn't want to be a tattletale. But Lucy had done a terrible thing.

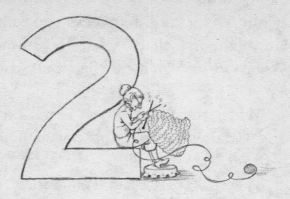

THE DAY after Henry Bigg's birthday
party, the Littles were together in their
living room. Granny Little was in her
rocking chair. She was knitting something she'd been working on for weeks.
Nobody knew what it was. Granny Little
was keeping it a secret. Whatever it was,
it was big.

Uncle Pete, cane in hand, was limping
back and forth in front of the fireplace.
Uncle Pete had been wounded in the
Mouse Invasion of '35. He always

clumped his cane loudly when he walked. "Granny," he said, "for weeks you've been knitting on that what-do-you-call-it. When are we going to find out what it is?"

"When the time comes, Peter Little," said Granny Little. "And not a moment before."

"Where's Dad?" said Tom Little. Tom was standing on his head in the corner of the room.

"Your father's been on the roof ever since the wind began blowing from the east," said Mrs. Little.

Tom somersaulted to a sitting position. "Is Cousin Dinky coming?"

"I wouldn't be surprised," said Mrs. Little. "He's been in the east for weeks, and the wind is finally blowing this way again."

"Oh goody!" Lucy clapped her hands. "I *love* it when Cousin Dinky comes. I hope he's been to Tina Small's house. She owes me a letter."

Cousin Dinky Little was Mr. Little's adventurous nephew. He had been all over and seen everything. He knew all the tiny people in the Big Valley.

Cousin Dinky was the only person in the Big Valley to travel from house to house. The others were afraid to go too far away from their homes. It was dangerous.

The nearest family to the Littles were the Smalls. A trip to the Smalls would take a whole day. There was danger every step of the way. They had to cross a road and get over a brook. There were animals everywhere.

Tiny families like the Littles, the Fines, the Smalls, the Crums, the Shorts, the Buttons, and all their kith and kin, lived all over the Big Valley. But they never got together.

There was one thing, however, that gave them a feeling of belonging to each other. It was Cousin Dinky Little. Cousin Dinky had visited every family at least twice. He had seen some of the families many times. Wherever Cousin Dinky went, he told news of other tiny people he had met on his travels. Through Cousin Dinky, many people who had never met got to know one another.

Someone was always giving Cousin Dinky a letter to carry to a friend. His pockets were stuffed with letters. Some of them weren't delivered for months. But nobody cared. They thought they were lucky to get letters delivered at all.

When Cousin Dinky first began his life of travel and adventure, he walked everywhere. He soon grew tired of that. The danger didn't bother him. In fact, he liked danger. But walking was so slow! Cousin Dinky wanted to go everywhere *fast*. So he built a glider.

He built the best glider he knew how. Then he practiced and practiced flying off the Biggs' roof. He had a few crashes, and he got a few scratches and bumps. But at last he became an expert glider pilot.

On still, calm days Cousin Dinky stayed put. Whenever the wind blew, he flew. And he always flew in the direction of the wind.

Cousin Dinky would glide with the wind until he came to a house where a tiny family lived. Then he would land and stay with them until the next windy day.

As soon as the wind shook the trees, Cousin Dinky would be off again. He'd look at his map and check the wind direction to decide where he would go.

But no matter what direction the wind blew, Cousin Dinky knew a tiny family was waiting for him.

"Isn't it wonderful how Cousin Dinky gets to meet all the tiny people?" said Lucy.

"I wish I were Cousin Dinky," said Tom.

"Well, *I* don't wish you were Cousin Dinky," Mrs. Little said. "Your cousin lives a very dangerous life."

"I was a lot like Dinky Little when I was younger," said Uncle Pete. He looked

at himself in the mirror over the fireplace. "He takes after me, don't you think?"

"I wish Cousin Dinky would teach me how to fly," Tom said. "Maybe I'll ask him if he comes."

"We'll hear no more of that, if you please, Tom," said Mrs. Little. "It's dangerous enough that you ride all over on the back of the Biggs' cat. Every time you go out on that cat, I hold my breath until you come back."

"Hildy's my friend," said Tom. "When I'm with her, I'm safer than when I'm home."

"Please," said Mrs. Little. "You're only ten years old. You don't know what you're saying."

"Oh, but he *does*, Mother," said Lucy. "He does!" Lucy rushed to her mother and hugged her. "Staying home all the time is terrible. Cousin Dinky knows *everyone*. He has friends *everywhere*.

And we — we're stuck here in this house."
Lucy began to cry. "Why, Tina Small is
probably my *best* friend, and I've never
even seen her!"

Uncle Pete limped over to Lucy. He
patted her on the back. "No tears, my
dear," he said. "You know my rule — no
tears in front of your uncle." He looked
hard at Mrs. Little. "For goodness' sake,
say something nice to her. Tell her what
we're having for dessert tonight."

"How can I do that?" said Mrs. Little.
"You know as well as I do that we eat
what the Biggs eat. And I have no idea
what Mrs. Bigg has planned for supper."
She gave Lucy a hug and a kiss.

THE WIND blew hard from the east all that day. Clouds hurried across the sky. Treetops fought the wind.

Mr. Little was standing on the Biggs' roof with Lucy and Tom. It was the first time Lucy's mother let her go up on the roof. "Try to stay close to the shelter of the chimney," said Mr. Little. "It's very windy up here. We don't want anyone losing his balance."

Tom looked over the edge of the roof. "And doing a nose dive into Mrs. Bigg's gooseberry bush," he added.

"Where is Cousin Dinky?" said Lucy. She looked at the sky.

"You'd think he'd be here by now if he were coming," said Tom. "The wind has been blowing for hours."

"He may have been all the way to the end of the Big Valley," said Mr. Little. "There are quite a few families between here and the eastern end of the Valley. And he has to pick up and drop off the mail at each house as he goes by."

"If he stops at every house," said Lucy. "How will he ever have time to get here today?"

"You know he doesn't *stop* at every house," said Tom. "He picks up the mail without landing."

"Right," said Mr. Little. He pointed to the end of the Biggs' TV antenna. "We loop the strap of our mail sack over the end of the antenna. Cousin Dinky glides in and yanks the sack off the antenna with a hook. It works beautifully."

"But how do we get *our* mail?" said Lucy.

"He drops it in the chimney," said Mr. Little.

"In the *chimney?*" said Lucy.

Mr. Little laughed. "It doesn't go down the chimney, Lucy," he said. "We've strung a net across the chimney. The net is just a few inches down from the top. It lets the smoke go up, and it keeps the letters from going down."

"But doesn't Cousin Dinky usually land at our house?" said Lucy.

"Well," said Mr. Little. "We're his closest relatives. He likes to stop off here."

"There's Cousin Dinky now!" shouted Tom.

Mr. Little and Lucy looked up. They saw a light blue glider coming toward them out of the eastern sky. The glider was flying low — almost as low as the trees at the edge of the Biggs' yard.

"He's too low," said Mr. Little. "Get higher, Dinky! Get up higher!" he shouted.

Suddenly the glider dived toward the trees. The Littles lost sight of it for a moment.

"There he is!" shouted Lucy.

"Wow!" said Tom. "He went *under* the trees!"

The glider rose in a long curve to the roof. As it drew near, two parachutes snapped open. The parachutes acted like a brake and made the glider slow down.

At the same time, the pilot threw out a fish-hook anchor tied to a piece of twine. The anchor caught on a shingle and the glider bounced to a landing.

Cousin Dinky leaped from the cockpit and helped the Littles tie the glider to the roof. When that was done, the four

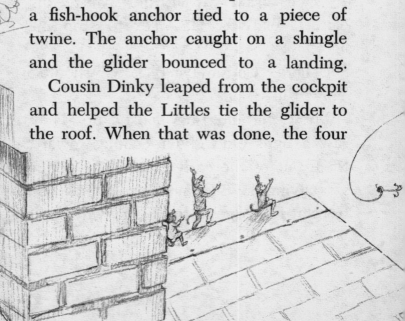

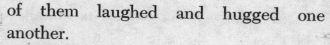

of them laughed and hugged one
another.

"One of my rougher landings," said
Cousin Dinky. "It's the wind. A little
faster than I like to fly in."

Mr. Little shook his head. "Dinky,"
he said. "You're going to get killed
someday landing like that. Isn't there a
better way?"

"If you mean isn't there a *safer* way,
Uncle Will," said Cousin Dinky, "sure
there's a safer way. I could land on that
air strip." He pointed to the Biggs'
driveway. "But when I want to take
off again, I'd have to get the glider up
on the roof anyway. Might as well land
here in the first place, eh?"

"Did you bring us any letters, Cousin
Dinky?" said Lucy.

"I did, Lucy, I did," said Cousin

Dinky. "If you people will help me get these sacks downstairs" — he reached into the cockpit of the glider and pulled out an armful of mail sacks — "I'll sort out your letters from the rest in a jiffy."

"Did I get a letter from Tina Small?" said Lucy.

"You did, you did," said Cousin Dinky. "I visited with the Smalls on my way down east." He reached into his large coat pocket. "I have it right here."

"Oh good!" said Lucy. She hugged Cousin Dinky. "You're wonderful, Cousin Dinky. I love it when you come."

"Now let's get out of this wind," said Mr. Little. "Dinky, you must be hungry."

"That's a true fact, Uncle Will," said Cousin Dinky. "Hungry's the word. And what I'm hungry for is Mrs. Bigg's cooking. No one in this part of the Valley can hold a candle to Mrs. Bigg when it comes to cooking."

"Come on," said Mr. Little. He looked at the sun in the west. "By this time the Biggs are about ready to eat dessert. If we hurry, we'll be just in time to take some leftovers."

"Hold everything!" said Cousin Dinky. "I almost forgot my guitar. I've learned a new song I want to sing to you. Tom, will you get the guitar for me? It's in the back of the glider behind the seat."

"Okay, Cousin Dinky," said Tom. But he didn't seem to be in a hurry to get the guitar. There was one thing Tom could never understand. How could a great man like Cousin Dinky have such a bad singing voice — and not know it?

"WOW!" said Cousin Dinky. "These chicken livers with pineapple are really delicious." He smacked his lips loudly. "May I have a wee bit more, Auntie?"

"You may have my share, Cousin Dinky," said Tom, "since you like it so much. Chicken livers make me gag."

"Tom," said Mrs. Little. "No one is interested in your gagging."

"It's amazing how things are the same as they always were," said Uncle Pete. "When I was a boy, chicken livers made *me* gag."

"I remember," said Granny Little.

"Most things have changed a lot since you were a boy," said Tom.

Lucy Little nodded.

"The most important things don't change," said Uncle Pete. "The way you children live is pretty much the same as I lived when I was a boy, as far as I can see."

"That's the trouble," said Tom. "Things have changed a lot, but we live the same old way."

"Tiny children may *live* the same," said Cousin Dinky, "but they're not the same."

"What do you mean, Cousin Dinky?" said Mrs. Little.

"In my travels I've met and talked to many children," said Cousin Dinky. "And I've found they're even different from when *I* was a boy. And that's not so long ago."

"How are they different?" said Mrs. Little.

"Tell us," said Mr. Little. "We're interested in what you've found out."

"I'll listen," said Uncle Pete. "But I'll tell you right now you're wrong."

"Shush, Peter Little," said Granny Little. "Maybe you can learn something new."

"If you'll hand me my guitar, Tom," said Cousin Dinky. "I'll sing a song that tells what I mean."

"You'll what?" said Uncle Pete.

Cousin Dinky didn't notice that almost all the Littles looked glum when he said he was going to sing. Granny Little, who was hard of hearing anyway, was the only one pleased.

"It's a song, Uncle Pete," said Cousin Dinky, "written by the little Crum girl, Betty."

"Great Scott!" said Uncle Pete. "I thought we were going to hear some *reasons* for what you believe."

"Let's listen, Uncle Pete," said Mr. Little. He leaned over and whispered, "We can just listen to the words, not the music."

"Music?" Uncle Pete grunted. "What music?"

Cousin Dinky began to sing:

While hiding in the walls, I watch
the bigger children's games.
They don't know I'm here, and they
don't even know my name.

If I had someone my size
to visit for a day,
I wouldn't have to make believe
a friend had come to play.

I'm not really happy just to
send my friend a letter.
If only I could meet her, we
could know each other better.

Then I would not have to play
the game of I'll pretend.
I would always know I had
a really, truly friend.

When Cousin Dinky was finished singing, Lucy was crying. "It's true!" she said. "Everything in the song is true. We don't have any friends."

"All we ever do is *watch* Henry Bigg and his friends," said Tom. "It's creepy. We know *all* about Henry and his friends . . . and they don't even know we're alive."

"They've been watching too much," said Mr. Little to Mrs. Little. "We'll have to set a time limit. It's no good for them to watch so much. We tiny people *must* have lives of our own. Tom and Lucy mustn't get too interested in the Biggs." He looked from one to another of the grownups. "There's always the danger that . . ."

"Do you mean . . . ?" said Uncle Pete.

"Yes," said Mr. Little. "Tom or Lucy might try to talk to Henry or write him a letter—something like that."

"Lucy has written Henry Bigg a letter

already," said Tom. "But I made her tear it up."

For a moment no one said anything. They all looked at Lucy.

"This is serious," said Uncle Pete.

"Lucy, I'm surprised," said Mrs. Little.

"I'm sorry, Mother," said Lucy. "But it was Henry's birthday and all. I won't do it again."

Mr. Little put his head in his hands. "My oh my," he said. "I never dreamed things were this bad with you children." He turned to his wife. "If Lucy does it once, she may do it again."

Mr. Little looked from Granny Little to Uncle Pete. "We've tried to bring up Tom and Lucy just as our parents brought us up. What did we do wrong?"

"Now, now," said Granny Little. "Don't be so hasty. They're good children."

Uncle Pete put his arm around Lucy. Suddenly Mrs. Little pointed a finger at Cousin Dinky. "Cousin Dinky," she said. "I think it's mostly *your* fault the children in the Valley are restless."

Cousin Dinky looked surprised.

"When Mr. Little and I were children, we hardly knew any boys and girls," said Mrs. Little. "And we certainly weren't able to send letters to anyone. But we were happy anyway. Now, because of you, children today are unhappy with the old ways."

"Now that I think of it, Dinky, your aunt is right," said Mr. Little. "You've been all over the Big Valley and you know everyone. The children don't seem to care how dangerous it is — they want to be like you."

"Bless you, Cousin Dinky," said Mrs. Little. "You can't help being the way you are—"

"And we love you the way you are," Granny Little said.

"Children need to play with other children, I suppose," Mrs. Little went on. "It's just that it's so dangerous."

"I've been thinking," said Cousin Dinky. "There's no reason why you shouldn't have a meeting of the four or five families close to you. It's not as dangerous as you think, Auntie. Honestly. And that way," Cousin Dinky looked at Lucy and smiled, "the children in the families would get to know one another. Then they'd be less likely to do foolish things," he blew Lucy a kiss, "like writing letters to Henry Bigg."

"Do you mean leave our home and travel overland? Just so our children can meet other children? No other reason?" said Mr. Little.

"Yes, I do mean that, Uncle Will," said Cousin Dinky. "It's the only way for the children to get to know one another."

"Oh dear," said Mrs. Little.

"Hold on there, Dinky," said Uncle Pete. "It's all right for adventurers like you or me to do such things, but for the women and children . . ."

"It's been sort of an unwritten rule," said Mr. Little, "that no tiny person leaves his home unless there's a great need or danger."

Granny Little stood up. "Rubbish!" she said. "Dinky is absolutely right, as usual. We can't go on doing things in the old ways. These children *need* to meet other children, and they *should*."

"Now, Granny," said Uncle Pete.

"I know what I'm talking about," said Granny Little. "Will said there should be a great *need* before tiny people leave their homes. Well, there is a need. It's as plain as water. I'm tired of all this scaredy-cat business." Granny Little sat down. "I haven't seen Zelda Short in twenty years. I love all of you, but I'd like to look at some other faces for a change."

"But, Granny," said Mr. Little. "Even if we decide that some of us should go, don't you think you're a little too . . . ah . . . er—"

"OLD!" said Granny Little. "Don't be afraid to say the word." She stood up. "Well, *I'm* not too old. I've got two good legs, don't I?"

"We could go on the Biggs' cat," said Tom. "She'll do anything I tell her."

"Oh good! Oh good!" said Lucy. "We're going."

Mr. Little looked at Mrs. Little. "This

is a foolish and dangerous idea, isn't it?" he said.

"Yes, it is," said Mrs. Little. She reached for her husband's hand. "And I'm scared. Because I keep thinking it's a wonderful idea, too."

"Everybody has gone mad," said Uncle Pete. "Absolutely mad."

Cousin Dinky reached into his big coat pocket. "I have my map right here," he said. He spread the map out over the table. "There are four families close by: the Crums, the Smalls, the Shorts, and the Buttons. The Smalls seem to be the family in the center — the easiest for all of you to get to."

All the Littles crowded around the map.

"Won't Tina Small be surprised," said Lucy. "I wonder what she looks like?"

DURING the next few weeks Cousin Dinky flew his glider back and forth among the Smalls, the Crums, the Shorts, the Buttons, and the Littles.

The Smalls were overjoyed at the idea of having a meeting of tiny families in their home. They set about making extra beds from some cigar boxes Mr. Small had been saving for years. And they finally got to work on that guest room they had been planning for the attic.

The Crum family were afraid to journey overland to the Smalls. Mr. and Mrs. Crum didn't think there was a good enough reason to face the hardship and dangers that might happen to them away from home. Cousin Dinky tried hard to get them to change their minds. "After all," he told them, "it was Betty who wrote the song that made everybody want to go."

"It's just a song, Dinky," said Mr. Crum. "We're not changing our way of life because of a song."

The Crum children were very disappointed.

The Shorts said they would come. Their oldest girl had been writing to the Small's oldest boy. They wanted very much to meet each other. They also had a boy Tom Little's age named Curt. He and Tom had been sending each other messages in code.

Mr. and Mrs. Button were the family nearest to the Smalls. They decided to come even though they had no children. "If it's your idea, Dinky," said Mr. Button, "I'm all for it."

The Buttons were one of the few tiny families in the valley who dared to visit their neighbors once in a while. Mr. and Mrs. Button came to visit the Smalls every summer. Over the years they had found the safest way to go.

The day set for the meeting was August the second. The night before, when everyone was packing, Granny Little finally showed the Littles what she had been knitting.

Ever since Tom Little had tamed Hildy the cat, the old woman had secretly wanted to ride her. So she had knitted a large double basket to be hung over the cat's back. "I didn't knit this contraption for the trip," said Granny Little. "But

now that it's finished, maybe we can use it."

The invention was tested and found workable. Mr. Little decided they should use it on the trip. Mrs. Little would ride in one basket on one side of the cat's back, and Granny Little would ride on the other side.

Tom would ride in his usual place on Hildy's neck. Or he would walk in front of the animal. Tom had tamed the cat by talking to it. He didn't want to get too far away from the cat's ears.

The big day arrived. The Littles were all set to go. They went over their plans with Cousin Dinky one last time.

"If you follow the route I've laid out for you," said Cousin Dinky, "there won't be any trouble. Remember, I've made many trips on foot in the Big Valley. Believe me, I know the safest way."

The Littles nodded.

Uncle Pete waved a sword made from one of Mrs. Bigg's needles. "There's nothing to worry about, Dinky," he said. "This sword is the best protection there is."

"Put that thing away before you scratch someone," said Granny Little.

"As I see it," said Mr. Little, "if we have to use our weapons, that will mean we haven't done things right."

"That's a true fact, Uncle Will," said Cousin Dinky. "This should be a peaceful, enjoyable trip."

"Nonsense!" said Uncle Pete. "If we really believed that, we wouldn't carry any weapons. I see you're all well armed."

It was true. The Littles were prepared for trouble. Mr. Little carried another needle sword. Tom Little was armed with a bow and arrows. Lucy carried some pepper — she thought the pepper would be a powerful weapon to use on an enemy. "It'll make him sneeze so much he won't be able to fight," she said. Mrs. Little was armed too. She carried her kitchen knife tied to her waist. In addition to all this, each Little carried a match stuck in his belt.

"Yes, Uncle Pete, we are armed," said Mrs. Little. "We are also carrying presents for our friends. I'd rather think about that."

Lucy Little giggled. "I can use my pepper for a present *or* a weapon, Uncle Pete," she said.

"I know you think your pepper's a powerful secret weapon, Lucy," said Uncle Pete. "Just make sure the wind is blowing the right way when you use it.

Your old uncle doesn't want to be seasoned."

All the Littles laughed.

"Speaking of the wind blowing the wrong way," said Cousin Dinky, "I'll be flying back and forth over your routes. There are four families to watch over. And I may not have the wind to my back when I need it. So if you do get into trouble," Cousin Dinky went on, "send up the red kite I made for you and keep it up. Each family has a red kite and a spool of thread."

"You did get the thread, didn't you, Lucy?" said Mrs. Little.

"I got it from Mrs. Bigg's sewing basket yesterday and gave it to Tom," said Lucy.

"It's in my pack," said Tom, "on Hildy, with the rest of the packs."

"Are you sure you can trust that cat?" said Cousin Dinky.

"Tom and the Biggs' cat are best friends," said Mrs. Little. She smiled at her son.

"Tom has a way with cats," said Mr. Little. "He tamed Hildy by talking to her. I wouldn't have believed it could be done. But I saw him do it with my own two eyes."

"And I still don't believe it," said Uncle Pete. "I wouldn't load my pack on that animal for all the tea in China. When that cat runs for home, at least one of us will have something left."

"Now, Peter," said Granny Little. "Just because Tom tamed the cat and proved you wrong, you can't admit it."

"Umph!" said Uncle Pete. "You'll see."

"Hildy will do a good job," said Mr. Little.

"You can't ever tell what a cat will do," said Uncle Pete.

THE LITTLES started out. Mr. Little led the way. Lucy was next. She wore new hiking boots and carried her pepper shaker. Tom walked in front of the cat. He talked to her all the time. Mrs. Little and Granny Little rode on either side of the cat in the knitted baskets.

Hildy the cat carried everyone's pack except Uncle Pete's. Uncle Pete was armed with a bow and arrows as well as his needle sword. He kept telling himself the trip was foolish. But if it was what his family wanted to do, he'd go along with it. And they just might need his help if there was trouble. Hadn't he been an expert bowman during the terrible Mouse Invasion of '35?

When the Littles were out of the house, Mr. Little held up his hand. "Stop here under this lilac bush," he said. "You, Tom — climb up the bush and see if the yard is clear to cross."

Just as Tom reached the top of the tall lilac bush, he heard a WHOOSH over his head. It was Cousin Dinky taking off in his glider from the Biggs' roof.

Tom wanted to cheer, but he stopped himself. The Biggs might hear him. Instead he waved wildly, shaking the top of the bush.

Cousin Dinky didn't see Tom until he circled around and flew back over the house. He waved at Tom by dipping the

glider's wings. Then he went over the trees and out of sight.

Tom could see most of the yard from the lilac bush. None of the Biggs was near.

It was Monday morning. Mrs. Bigg would be in the house doing her laundry. Mr. Bigg was at work. The Bigg to watch out for was Henry. He might be any-where around the house.

And any minute Henry and his friends might run through the yard like a herd of elephants. Whenever Henry and his friends stormed into the house, Mrs. Bigg would say, "Henry! I don't want anyone running in the house. If you must act like a herd of elephants, do it in the yard. That's what the yard is for."

Tom looked over the yard and decided the coast was clear.

Cousin Dinky had told the Littles how to cross the yard. "Go from the lilac bush to the black walnut tree," he said. "Then go through the flower garden in the yard next door." Cousin Dinky told the Littles to go through flower gardens whenever they could. He said people taught their pets to stay out of them.

"I hope Cousin Dinky knows what he's talking about," thought Tom Little. Tom was worried about the mean-looking dog next door. He hoped the dog had been taught to stay out of the flower garden.

Tom couldn't see where the Smalls lived from the lilac bush. He knew where the house was, though, because he had seen it from the Biggs' rooftop. There was a woods between the two houses.

Cousin Dinky had never been in the woods. He said it was probably full of wild animals. "A good place to stay away from," he said. So Cousin Dinky had chosen a way that went around the woods. It was longer, he said, but safer, because it kept to the yards and gardens.

Tom took one more long look, to make sure no one was in the yard. Then he climbed down the lilac bush and jumped onto Hildy's neck. "I didn't see anyone," he told his father.

"That's a long piece of yard to cross over," said Mr. Little. "Cousin Dinky says it's the worst part of the trip. After this the rest is easy, he says. Let's try to move extra fast until we get to the walnut tree way at the back of the yard."

"Let's go," said Uncle Pete. "Let's get the show on the road."

Mr. Little raised his hand and signaled his family to follow him. They moved out from under the lilac bush into the bright sunlight.

The band of tiny people was halfway to the walnut tree when they heard yelling from the other side of the house. It was Henry Bigg and some of his friends.

"Good heavens!" said Mr. Little. "It sounds like they're coming this way."

Henry Bigg's voice could be heard above the rest, "I get to pitch, you guys."

"Aw, just because you have the best yard for playing baseball," said one of the boys, "you think you can tell us what to do."

The voices were growing louder.

"This is their ball field," said Tom.

"I've watched them play here a thousand times."

Mr. Little stopped in the middle of the yard. He looked to the right and left. "I wish you'd told us that before," he said.

"Let Henry pitch," called another boy. "He's got a good screwball."

The boys came around the corner of the house. They were tossing a baseball back and forth as they ran into the yard.

"Everybody up on Hildy's back!" said Mr. Little. He grabbed the loose skin of the cat and pulled himself up. Tom leaned down from Hildy's neck, took Lucy's hand, and pulled her up.

"Oh dear," said Mrs. Little. "Hold tight, Granny."

Uncle Pete, in his hurry, grabbed Hildy by the tail. "Mee-ow!" Hildy started to slink toward the woods. Uncle Pete finally got on her back.

"No, Hildy! No!" said Tom. "This

way." He pushed and prodded the animal, turning her head by pulling her ears gently. Suddenly the baseball spun through the air, bounced, and hit the cat in the side. "EEEEEooooowwwww!"

"Hey, you dummy," yelled Henry Bigg. "You hit my cat."

That was the last thing the Littles heard as Hildy ran from the yard and into the woods.

WHEN Hildy finally stopped running, the Littles were deep in the woods. Mr. Little and Tom climbed down from the cat.

"You can open your eyes now, Mother," said Tom. "We've stopped."

"Oh dear," said Mrs. Little. "Oh dear."

Mr. Little helped Mrs. Little and Granny Little out of their baskets.

"I don't want a ride like that again soon," said Mr. Little.

"We lost one of our packs," said Granny Little. "It got stuck on a bush back yonder."

Tom began to run. "I'll get it."

"Hold it, Tom," said Mr. Little. "We're in the woods now. We'd better stick together."

All the Littles looked around them at the woods.

"Look!" said Lucy. She pointed straight up. "The trees. See how they make a roof of leaves way high up. Aren't they beautiful?"

"Beautiful, my foot," said Uncle Pete. "We're in trouble. And all because of that doggone cat."

"It's not Hildy's fault," said Tom.

"That cat saved us from being trampled to death," said Granny Little.

Tom walked over to where Hildy was lying down, licking her paw. "She got mixed up, that's all," he said. "Oh, oh! There's a cut on her paw."

The Littles crowded around Hildy. Sure enough, she had a deep cut in the pad of her left forepaw.

"Poor Hildy-cat," said Lucy. She leaned against the wounded cat and whispered in her ear.

"Well — that's that," said Mr. Little. "Hildy can't go on with a cut paw."

"Listen," said Tom. "What's that?"

"It's Henry Bigg again," said Mr. Little.

"They must be looking for Hildy," said Tom.

"Quick!" said Mr. Little. "Get the packs and the bags off Hildy."

The Littles piled all over one another in their hurry. Then they ran under the nearest bush, dragging everything with them.

"Here, Hildy," called Henry Bigg. He was almost there.

Hildy tried to climb under the bush with the Littles.

"Talk to her, Tom!" said Mr. Little.

"No, Hildy," said Tom. "Go with Henry."

The cat gave Tom a puzzled look.

"Go!" said Tom.

"Hey — there she is, trying to crawl under a bush," said one of Henry's friends.

"Hey, Hildy — come here," said Henry.

The cat turned away from the bush and limped toward Henry.

"Aw, she's hurt," said Henry. He ran to Hildy and scooped her up in his arms. "She's been hurt. I told you guys she was hurt."

The three boys looked the cat over.

"It's her foot," said Henry. "She has a bad cut. C'mon, you guys — my mom will know what to do." He ran with the cat back toward his house.

Mr. Little sat down on the pile of packs. "Well," he said. He took a deep breath. "We have a choice. We can go back to the Biggs' house and start over, or we can . . ."

"Push on!" finished Uncle Pete. "We're halfway through the woods already."

"There's danger either way," said Mr. Little.

"Do we know the way?" Mrs. Little asked.

"Of course," said Uncle Pete. "We came from *that* way, and we have to go *that* way." He pointed with his cane.

"I agree with Uncle Pete that we are probably halfway into the woods," said Mr. Little.

"We came quite a distance," said Granny Little.

"I had my eyes closed," said Mrs. Little.

"I watched every step of the way," said Granny Little.

"Sorry about your baskets, Granny," said Mr. Little. "We're going to have to leave them behind."

"I hope Hildy will be okay," said Tom.

"I don't care much for cats," said Uncle Pete, "but I sure hate to see that poor animal hurt."

"All right," said Mr. Little. "Let's get these packs on and get going. I'll carry yours, Granny."

"Shouldn't we try to find the path?" Tom said. "I've heard Henry say it goes through the woods to the road."

"Tom and I could scout around for the path," said Uncle Pete. "It may take a little time. I think the ladies should stay here and save their strength."

"You said we should stay together, Will," said Mrs. Little.

"Uncle Pete has a point," said Mr. Little. "It may take some time to find the path."

"Tom and I will circle around and come back every now and then to check with you," said Uncle Pete.

Uncle Pete and Tom moved off through the underbrush. The walking was rough. They had to go around weeds and thick, wild bushes. It took a long time to go a short way.

"We'll *have* to find the path," said Uncle Pete, "or it'll take us a month of Sundays to get out of these woods."

At last they found the path. Uncle Pete stood in the middle of the path and leaned on his cane. "This is a sight for sore eyes," he said. The path was wide and seemed to go on forever.

"It's like a road for tiny people," said Tom. "It's as though someone made it especially for us."

They hurried back to get the others. But when they got to the place, there was no one in sight.

"WHERE are they?" said Tom Little. "This is the right place, isn't it?" He looked around.

Uncle Pete got out his needle sword. "It's the right place, all right," he said. "They're just not here." He ran over to the bush where the Littles had been waiting. "Look! Here's one of the packs. They must have left in a hurry."

Tom found some arrows. "Maybe there's been a fight, Uncle Pete," he said. "Oh golly, what'll we do?"

"Keep your head, boy," said Uncle Pete. "They're probably hiding somewhere in a better spot." He slapped his sword against his leg. "I was a fool to leave them in this dumb place. They could be attacked from any direction."

"Look!" Tom pointed to the ground. "They went this way." There were footprints in the soft dirt.

"Good boy!" said Uncle Pete. "Let's go!" He limped off, keeping an eye to the ground.

Tom drew an arrow from his quiver. He fixed it to his bow and followed his uncle.

It was tough going. They had to climb over pebbles and twigs. The thick grasses were over their heads. Uncle Pete almost got trapped in a mudhole filled with wet, rotting leaves. Finally they came to a small clearing. There was a large rock ahead.

"If I were in Will's shoes," said Uncle Pete. "I'd go to that rock. With that behind you, you'd stand a chance." He broke into a limping run. "C'mon!"

"Wait, Uncle Pete!" Tom yelled. "Shouldn't we sneak up on it?"

But Uncle Pete wasn't listening. If his family was in danger some place, he would save them. "Hold on, Will!" he yelled. "I'm coming!" Suddenly a bird about ten inches long dropped down on top of him. It got its claws into Uncle Pete's pack and started to lift him off the ground.

Tom shot an arrow. It missed. He used his bow like a bat and beat at the bird until Uncle Pete could slip his pack off.

Another bird attacked them. Its wings beat hard, scattering the loose dirt and leaves.

Uncle Pete struck at the second bird with his needle sword. "They're sparrow hawks!" he yelled. "Don't let them get a grip on you."

Mr. Little ran out from the shelter of the big rock and joined the fight. The three Littles stood back to back. They hit at the hawks with swords and bows. The birds attacked again and again. Feathers flew.

Lucy ran toward them, her pepper shaker raised over her head. Mrs. Little ran after her and pulled her back.

Suddenly a great black and white skunk waddled out of the woods. It headed for the fighters. When the skunk got close by, it began hissing and stamping its forefeet.

The sparrow hawks stopped attacking the Littles and flew off. The Littles turned to face the new danger. The skunk stood over them.

"Hallo there!" said a voice. "What are you doing? Bird hunting?"

"What's that?" said Mr. Little. The voice seemed to come from the animal.

Then he saw the skunk wasn't alone. High up on the skunk's neck was a tiny man!

"My goodness!" said Mr. Little.

"Great jumping lizards!" said Uncle Pete.

The man said something to the skunk.

The skunk lowered its head and the man slid off onto the ground. "I woulda been here sooner, but old skunk here was asleep," he said.

Uncle Pete shook the man's hand. "We were in a mess," he said. He was breathing hard. "My name's Peter Little . . . this is my nephew, Will Little . . . and his son Tom."

The man shook hands with Mr. Little and Tom.

"I'm Stubby Speck," he said. "What part of the woods do you folks come from?"

"We don't live in the woods, Mr. Speck," said Mr. Little.

"We didn't know any tiny people lived in the woods,'" said Uncle Pete.

Stubby Speck spoke slowly. "Then you folks must live . . . in . . . in a HOUSE!"

"As a matter of fact, we do," said Mr. Little.

"Well I'll be —" said Stubby Speck.

"House Tinies! Why, you're House Tinies!"

"House Tinies?" said Tom. He looked at his father. "Are we House Tinies, Dad?"

Stubby Speck walked around and around the Littles, looking them over. "I swear," he said, "you look just like Wood Tinies." He stopped and scratched his head. "You do talk kinda different, though."

Granny Little, Mrs. Little, and Lucy came out from behind the rock where they had been hiding. Mr. Little ran to them. "Are you all right?" he asked.

"Of course we're all right," said Granny Little. "You were the ones in trouble."

Mr. Little introduced Stubby Speck to the rest of his family.

"Pleased to meet you, ma'am," said Stubby Speck to the two ladies. "And you, miss," he said to Lucy.

He took off his hat and bowed.

"Mr. Speck," said Granny Little. "You probably saved our lives."

"Well now," said Stubby Speck. "I have a million questions to ask you folks. What are you doing in the woods? . . . Where are you going? . . . What's it like living in a house? . . . and so forth and so on."

Mr. Speck looked up at the sun. "It's about noon," he said. He rubbed his round, hard belly and took a deep breath. "Smell that? It's mushroom pie. Would you have lunch with me and my folks? My youngsters would sure like that."

At the word "youngsters," Lucy and Tom began jumping up and down and hugging each other.

"We'd enjoy that very much, Mr. Speck," said Mr. Little. "Tom and Lucy are dying to meet other tiny children."

"Your wife does her own cooking?" said Mrs. Little.

"She does many things well, ma'am," said Stubby Speck, "but cooking is the jewel in her crown."

"Is your house nearby?" said Mr. Little.

Mr. Speck laughed. "We don't call it a house," he said. "We call it a tree."

"You live in a tree?" said Tom. "Boy, that's great!"

THE STUBBY Speck family lived in the lowest branch of a giant oak tree. Steps had been cut into the bark of the great tree. They went around and around the trunk until they came to the lowest branch. The stairway looked like part of the tree. The Littles did not even see the stairs until Mr. Speck pointed them out.

The Littles followed their new friend up the long stairway. "My great-great-granddaddy dug out our eight rooms in this tree many years ago," said Mr. Speck.

Tom pointed to the lowest branch. "What's that?" he said. "What are those round shiny things in the tree?"

"They're my windows, son," said Mr. Speck. "I made them myself from the bottoms of bottles that floated into the woods on the brook."

"Wonderful!" said Mr. Little.

Mr. Speck spoke again, "The bark shutters are made so they'll swing shut to hide the windows," he said. "Sometimes Henry Bigg and his friends climb on our tree. When they do, we just shut everything up tight and wait for the boys to go away."

Later, the Littles and the Specks had lunch in the largest room in the tree. Sunlight streamed through the colored bottle windows. A long oak table grew right out of the floor. It was part of the living tree.

The table was covered with good

things to eat in wooden dishes. There was mushroom pie, dandelion green salad, sassafras tea sweetened with honey, and blackberries for dessert.

Lucy and Tom sat at one end of the table with the Specks' two daughters. The oldest girl, Annie, was a year older than Tom Little. Tom soon found out that Annie didn't know *anything*. She wanted to know all about Henry Bigg. She had seen Henry and his friends playing in the woods from time to time. Whenever Tom answered one of her questions, she asked another. Did Henry have a sister? What was his room like? How tall was he really?

Finally Tom said, "We don't watch the Biggs all the time. We Littles have lives of our own."

The youngest Speck girl, Janie, was Lucy Little's age exactly. They quickly became best friends for life. "Oh, you're *so* lucky," Lucy whispered to Janie, "having a *sister*."

"I think you're lucky having a brother," Janie whispered back.

They both went into a fit of giggling.

Mrs. Little was delighted.

Uncle Pete spoke, "Mr. Speck, I'm *astounded* by you people and this place of yours."

"Astounded?" said Mr. Speck. "What do you mean?"

"Why, you people live here in the woods winter and summer," said Uncle Pete. "And as far as I can see, you don't get any help from anyone."

"I've been wondering myself," said Mr. Little, "how you get along by yourselves. We depend on the Biggs for so many things. Of course we *help* them too. We do electrical repair work in the walls. And we keep the outside water pipes from freezing during the winter." Mr. Little smiled. "I suppose the Littles and the Biggs sort of help each other. But you Specks get no help from anyone. How do you do it?"

"I never gave it much thought," said Mr. Speck. "I suppose we do it because we have to." He turned to his wife. "How do we do it, Mrs. Speck?"

"I think you're right, as usual, Mr. Speck," said Mrs. Speck. "We do it because we have to."

Mr. Speck nodded. "Smart woman," he said.

"We have to work hard," Mrs. Speck

went on. "There's always winter coming on in the woods."

"Even in the spring," said Mr. Speck, "we're thinking about the next winter. How we've got to do this or we've got to do that before next winter."

"There's always plenty to do, even for the youngsters," said Mrs. Speck. "But we Specks are strong. We love to work."

"There's one thing that makes everything work out fine," said Mr. Speck. "And I think . . . no, I *know* it's the most important thing."

Mrs. Speck rapped on the table with her spoon. "Attention, everyone!" she said. "Mr. Speck is talking about something *important*. I think I know what it is, and I want you all to hear it."

Mr. Speck nodded at Mrs. Speck. "Thank you, Mrs. Speck. As I was saying, there's no question in my mind but that the most important thing is" — he looked around the table — "Mrs. Speck's cooking. My wife is a great cook!"

Everyone laughed. There were shouts of, "Yes! Yes! Agreed!"

Stubby Speck held up his hand. "I wish you all wouldn't laugh about such a serious thing as cooking," he said. "With the good Mrs. Speck's cooking in me, I can do anything . . . and I mean *anything!*"

The Littles and the Specks talked for two hours. Even though the two families had never met before, they had much to tell each other. After a while, the Specks knew something of what it was like to live in a house. And the Littles heard and saw for themselves what living in the woods was like.

"I'm wondering," said Mr. Little, "why we never heard there were tiny people living in the woods."

"You never got told, that's why," said

Mr. Speck. "My great-great-granddaddy used to live in a house just like you folks. But he had two of them burn down over his head. The last time he just got up and walked into the woods and never came back."

"You told us there were other families living in the woods," said Mr. Little. "How did they get here?"

"Kinda the same way," said Mr. Speck. "Every now and then a tiny family just gets tired of living with big people. There must be something in tinies that makes them head for the woods when they get tired of house living."

"There hasn't been a new family of tinies come into the woods in sixty years," said Mrs. Speck. She smiled at her guests. "House living must be getting better."

Finally it was time to leave. Mr. Speck woke up his skunk. He and the skunk would take the Littles down the path as far as the brook. "That's close to the big people's road," he said. "If you follow the brook the short distance to the road, you can cross over on the bridge."

Mr. Speck shook his head. "I won't take you to the road, because someone might shoot at my skunk. Some crazy big people will shoot at anything that moves."

Mr. Speck went into the woods and found Granny Little's knitted baskets. He helped Mr. Little strap them on the skunk. Granny and Mrs. Little would ride in the baskets again.

The Specks and the Littles said their good-byes. Each family said it would never forget the other. Each promised it would come and visit.

Granny Little and Mrs. Little got into their baskets. The rest of the Littles climbed up on the skunk's broad back. Stubby Speck said something in the skunk's ear, and the animal walked slowly off through the underbrush. The two families waved until they were out of sight.

Mr. Speck pointed out the interesting things to look at on the trip. The last of the day lilies were in bloom. They were like bright orange lights in the sunny places of the woods. A maple tree was the home of another tiny family. Animals got out of the way quickly when they saw the skunk.

They came to the brook. It was about four feet wide and ten inches deep. The water moved swiftly.

The Littles could see the bridge through the trees. "Cross at the bridge," said Stubby Speck, "and you won't have to cross here and get wet."

"Mr. Speck," said Granny Little, "will

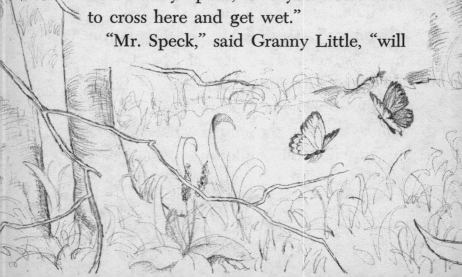

you keep the knitted baskets as a present from us?"

"I sure will, ma'am. Thank you kindly," said Mr. Speck. "My missus will love those baskets. Old skunk waddles a bit too much for her. She has a hard time staying on him."

The Littles thanked Mr. Speck. Everyone shook his hand. Mr. Speck took off his hat and bowed. Then he mounted his skunk and in a few moments he was out of sight.

THE LITTLES walked slowly along
the bank of the brook. Lucy talked
on and on about Janie Speck. She
decided to ask Cousin Dinky if he would
get mail to Janie. "He'll do it," she said.
"He can do anything."

They were a few minutes' walk from
the bridge when Mrs. Little grabbed her
husband's arm. "What's that?" she said.
Just ahead of the Littles, on the other
side of the brook, was a weasel. The
weasel and the Littles saw each other at
the same time.

Mr. Little knew they would never make it to the bridge even if they ran. He looked around for some place to hide his family. There was only a big bush nearby.

The weasel jumped into the brook. It swam rapidly across.

"Hurry!" yelled Mr. Little. "Make a ring of dried leaves and twigs around this bush — anything that'll burn." The Littles obeyed him at once.

"Use your matches!" said Mr. Little. He struck his match on a rock.

The weasel ran up the steep bank of the brook. Water streamed from its sleek body.

The other Littles lighted their matches from Mr. Little's match. The flaming matches frightened the weasel. It held back.

The leaves and twigs burst into flame around the bush.

The Littles stood within the circle of fire and shot arrows at the weasel. Some of them struck the ground near the animal. It ran back a few feet, but it wouldn't leave.

Mr. Little could see that they didn't have enough twigs and leaves to keep the fire burning for long. He looked around, searching for a way to escape.

"We're going to run out of dried stuff for this fire in a hurry," said Uncle Pete.

"I know, I know," said Mr. Little.

"Why don't we climb the bush, Daddy?" said Lucy. She was helping her uncle pile up fuel for the fire.

"That wouldn't stop the weasel," said Mr. Little. "It would climb after us."

Tom was looking at the bush. "See that branch that goes out over the brook, Dad?" he said.

Mr. Little nodded.

"I could climb onto the branch and jump into the brook. If the weasel didn't see me, I could make it down to the Smalls and get help."

Mr. Little looked at the branch carefully. "You could, Tom," he said. "You're lighter than I am." Then he looked outside the circle of fire. The weasel was still crouched, waiting. "Do it, Tom!" he said. "But for heaven's sake, do it quickly, boy."

Tom Little pulled off his pack and began climbing the bush.

Mrs. Little, who, along with Granny Little, had been feeding the fire, saw her son start up the bush. "Where's Tom going?" she shouted. "Tom — come back!"

Mr. Little rushed over to his wife. He put his arm around her. "I've sent Tom for help," he said.

"Oh no!" said Mrs. Little.

"Listen, everybody!" shouted Mr. Little. "Tom is going to get help. We don't want the weasel to see him. Make a lot of noise! Jump up and down! If the weasel is watching us, it may not see what Tom is doing."

"What's Tom doing?" said Mrs. Little.

"Yell, everyone! Yell!" screamed Mr. Little. He jumped up and down, shouting and waving his arms.

Tom crawled slowly out onto the branch over the brook. Below him, his family was making a terrible racket. The branch became thinner and thinner. It bent under the boy's weight. Tom Little closed his eyes and dropped into space.

COUSIN Dinky Little was worried. He had not seen the Littles since he had dipped his glider's wings at Tom early that morning. It was now late afternoon.

Cousin Dinky decided they must be in trouble some place. But where? Why didn't they send up the red kite he had given them?

Everything had worked well with the other families. The Buttons came to the Smalls first. The Shorts walked in a few hours later.

Right this minute the Short and Small

children were having a wonderful time together. The grownups, of course, couldn't enjoy themselves. They were too worried about the Littles.

Cousin Dinky stood on the roof of the Smalls' house. The sun was low in the sky. Cousin Dinky hoped there was time for one more trip in his glider before dark.

Luckily, the wind was still blowing. But Cousin Dinky knew it would drop off around sunset. For some reason it always did.

He climbed into the cockpit of his glider and pulled in the fish-hook anchor. The light glider coasted down the steep roof, picking up speed. It took to the air. The glider circled out over the brook which ran at the side of the house. It climbed higher.

Something was moving down on the bank of the brook. Cousin Dinky saw it out of the corner of his eye. It was one of the tiny people! He dipped the glider to get a better look. Someone was lying half out of the water.

The glider pilot lowered the flaps on the wings of his glider. It dropped quickly. He brought the glider down to a landing on the road.

Cousin Dinky scrambled down the bank of the brook. He found Tom Little. The boy was trying to stand up.

"Tom!" said Cousin Dinky. "What in the world happened? Where is everybody?"

"A weasel," said Tom. "Weasel . . . everybody trapped." He was breathing hard. "Need help . . . fast."

"Where?" said Cousin Dinky. "Where, Tom?"

"That way!" said Tom. "I'll show you." Tom tried to walk. He tripped and fell down.

"Never mind showing me," said Cousin Dinky. He picked Tom up. "You'd never make it. We've got to get help."

Cousin Dinky ran with Tom in his arms to the Smalls' rooms in the walls of the house. He told the families what had happened. In a jiffy the Smalls, the Shorts, and the Buttons had armed themselves and were running to help the Littles.

When they got to the bridge, they saw the Littles coming out of the woods! Mr. Little and Uncle Pete were carrying Lucy Little on their shoulders. Mrs. Little and Granny Little were laughing. The two men were cheering, "Hip, hip hooray for Lucy!"

The four families met in the middle of the bridge. "What happened, Uncle Will?" said Cousin Dinky. "Tom said you were trapped by a weasel."

Everybody talked at once. Above the happy mix-up, Lucy Little had a wide smile on her face.

"Lucy saved us!" shouted Mr. Little.

"She used her secret weapon!" yelled Uncle Pete, and then he sneezed.

"Bless you, Uncle Pete," said Cousin Dinky. "What happened to you people? We were all terribly worried. Now you come parading out of the woods as though you'd been on a picnic."

Mr. Little stood in the middle of the bridge and told the story of their adventures. "And when Tom climbed the bush," he said, "we didn't know that Lucy climbed right up after him. We were so busy jumping up and down and yelling, we never saw Lucy until she was way up on a branch right over the weasel."

"Then the weasel saw her," said Uncle Pete. "It jumped at her, trying to knock her out of the bush."

Mr. Little looked up at his daughter. "Tell them, honey," he said. "Tell them what you did then."

"I took the top off my pepper shaker," said Lucy, "and poured pepper on the weasel."

The tiny people gasped. Then they began to laugh.

"When last seen," Uncle Pete shouted, "Mr. Weasel was rubbing his eyes, sneezing, and going around in circles."

"There's a car coming!" Mr. Small shouted. "Get off the bridge!" Everyone ran helter-skelter to the side of the road.

"It's the master of the house," said Mr. Small. "They'll be eating soon. Come, everyone, let's find out what we're having for dinner."

Granny Little took an old lady by the arm. "Aren't you Zelda Short?" she asked.

"I am," said the old lady.

"I have a lot to tell you, Zelda," said Granny Little. "Let's go into the house where we can talk."

"I'm Tina Small," said a girl to Lucy. "Your brother's in the house. He's okay."

"I knew you were Tina," said Lucy.

"How'd you know?"

"I don't know—I just knew."

And so began the first annual meeting of the tiny people of the Big Valley.